QUEST FOR ANSWERS

A SHORT STORY EXPLORING CONNECTIONS BETWEEN INDIAN AND GREEK MYTHOLOGY

SRIVISHNU RAMACHANDRAN

To my grandparents –

the ones who instilled a passion for mythology in me

Contents

Preface

I've always been in love with mythology. Ever since I was young, I would read books and books on Indian, Greek, Norse and Egyptian mythology. The magic of the old world, the richness of the characters, and the deeds they did - it was all jaw-dropping for me.

Growing up, Rick Riordan and his mythological series were my constant companions. On the side, reenactments of the Mahabaratha or the Ramayanam were always on the TV.

To touch upon this love, this passion I had as a voracious reader, I'd always wanted to make a book of my own. A personal dream, something I wanted to do before I left for college. Years went by and I've only taken steps now, a year before I graduate. But better late then never right?

This book is a short story meant to explore the parallels between the worlds of Indian and Greek stories, a light tale that reveals the deep connections rooted in their respective histories.

In a way, I see myself in Shiv. A young man captivated by myths and legends since his youth, secretely hoping they're all real.

And of course, this is a purely fictional tale - my first step as an author.

I sincerely hope you enjoy this story.

CHAPTER ONE

The Beginning

"*Patti*, I want more!" His eyes, brimming with longing, peered upwards.

"Not now *kanna*, go eat now." Her smile was a weary one - old age did no one any favours.

The boy stuck his chin out, not budging from his grandma's legs.

"Please *patti*, I want more stories!" His eyes were sparkling, captivated with stories of old.

Spices wafted through the air as the aromatic flavours spread their tendrils, calling the boy to eat them. But to no avail. He was lost in the world of myths and legends his grandma had crafted for him, nurtured for years.

It was midday in Chennai, the sweltering heat and humidity driven out by the shade of decades-old banyan trees and numerous table fans. The two were situated in the courtyard, chirping and cawing a constant lullaby.

A rocking chair was occupied by the elderly lady, and at her feet was her grandson. A runt of a kid, our hero was stubbornly grasping the chair, refusing to go. Toys littered the space, thrown in the multitude of emotions kids are subject to. Food was being set out in the distance: *sambar, rice, rasam, khichdi* - a magnanimous feast indeed. But even the sweet, oh divine, smell of the *payasam* could not deter our hero. He was on a mission, a mission that would satiate his thirst for stories.

She huffed out a sigh of exasperation, now irritated.

"What has your mother taught you? Pestering me day and night," she grumbled.

"Alright, listen closely. Last tale and you go bother someone else, Shiv. Promise?"

"Yes *patti!*" The boy sat in attention, rapt, as the tale began.

"There was once a god living with humans, defeating monsters and keeping *Brindavan* safe from demons. The scariest monster was the many headed ..."

"...snake!"

The little girl squealed in glee as her grandfather tickled her incessantly.

"*Papu*, stop!" The girl squirmed and tried to break free, to no avail.

"*Herakles* crushed many monsters, but it was the many-headed hydra which scared him the most..." he continued with his tale, a state of quiet descending upon the child.

Out on the field, cows lolled about in the harsh, morning sun. A gentle breeze wafted through the farm, rustling dead leaves in its wake. Athens had been blessed by a cool climate this summer.

A dilapidated farmhouse oversaw the fields, consisting of a rocking chair occupied by an elderly man, swaying rhythmically. A girl of 8 sat beneath his feet, absorbed by the words he uttered, absorbed into a world of myths and legends.

"Eventually, with the help of his nephew, he defeated the monster with smartness and fire, burning each cut head so they didn't grow back," the grandpa continued, his eyes foreboding and eerie.

"Woah…"

"Woah indeed my little Alexandra. Now go play with the cows; my throat hurts," he grumbled.

With a tight hug and an exuberant kiss, she ran towards the drowsy cows, and the grandpa returned to napping with a smile on his haggard face.

"Rest your eyes for once, *pa*."

Lying on the sofa, butt hoisted in the air, Shiv was staring intently at the worn pages, too absorbed to even register her words.

His grandma let out a weary sigh and hobbled towards him. When Shiv started reading, nothing could sway him. She considered lifting him, but her now 10 year old grandson was a bit on the chubby side.

"Come on now, go out and play for a bit."

Disgruntled, he turned away from her, eyes still glued to Percy Jackson's exploits.

Chuckling, slowly turning into a raspy cough, she sat down next to him, stroking his unkempt hair.

"Bye, *patti*."

18 year old Shiv looked on as his grandmother beckoned him to approach her, her frail body painfully shaking with

every breath taken.

Holding in the tears, holding in the waterfall that he knew would never cease, he hugged her as tight as he could, for the last time.

He slowly walked towards the terminal, his university acceptance letter stuffed in his jacket pocket, as he bid a final farewell to his childhood.

"This is the pre-boarding announcement for flight 14J to Athens, Greece."

CHAPTER TWO

The Journey

13:00, Athens, Greece.

He was here. The cradle of Western civilization. Home to millenia-old ways of thought, art, literature: he was finally here. Stepping onto the tarmac, Shiv hadn't realised he was holding his breath. The tales of Hercules, The Minotaur, Perseus: he was finally in Greece.

Shouldering his straining duffel bag, he stepped out into the bustling image seen outside every airport - taxi drivers yelling to get the attraction of tourists, tour guides eyeing potential victims, buses tooting to hurry gossiping passengers on - how he had missed land. It had been a long flight.

As he adjusted himself on the tattered leather seats in a taxi, he looked out at the city looming large on the horizon, the Parthenon basking in the midday rays.

"Where to, *filo*?"

Click.

The yellow light cast a soft glow.

My room for the next 4 years, Shiv thought.

The light revealed a neat, compact room with sparse furniture. A glossy table, an office chair, a narrow bed and a bedside desk.

It'll do I guess.

Dumping his backpack on the table, he laid down on the mattress and stared at the ceiling.

As he watched solemnly, a spotted lizard scampered across, darting erratically. An alarmingly large size, but Shiv was tuned out. His mind was back in Chennai, back in the cool shade from the banyan trees. Back with his *patti*.

He shook his head and buried his face on the bed.

No, no, no.

He needed to go out and clear his head. With a sigh and a grunt, he heaved himself off the bed and put on his shoes.

"7 Zeus' for 12 euros!"

"2 Athena's for the price of one!"

Surging shopkeepers clamoured for attention, clamoured for the gaze of a tourist to fall on their wares. It was impossible to remain in place. Jostling tourists wormed through the crowd, creating a current of sweaty bodies throughout the marketplace.

Shiv's neck craned to break free of this river, to find land, to find escape before he was swept aside. What had started as a search for some decorations for his dorm had turned into a fight for survival. He really should have checked the popular hours for this market.

There it was. Casting an eerie glow in the sunlight, was a mosaic table lamp, narrating the tale of a hero slaying a monster. It had caught his eye when he had entered; the collection of broken pieces crucial to filling the hole in his bedside table. As he staggered towards it, bodies and bodies piling against him, it took him every ounce of his energy in his wiry body to not be swept away.

Holding the lamp in his hands, he felt it.

Just right.

"You break it, you buy it," said a voice behind the table slyly.

"How much?"

"8 euros."

An exorbitant price, but he was too tired to haggle. He handed the money without complaint.

"And here we have the legendary Hydra. As we can see, this multi-headed monster terrorized many…"

Patti ma. How he loved her tales of old, tales of monsters and myths. His ears perked as he listened on to this distant voice. He edged slowly towards the tour guide; a huddle of blank eyes were staring back at her.

"Herakles, or commonly known as Hercules, was one blessed by the gods. Although at his birth, the queen of the gods sent snakes to kill him as a child…"

"The evil uncle Kansa sent monsters and demons to kill Krishna as a child…"

Sunlight greeted him as he stepped onto the street. A huddle of indistinguishable tourists had encircled a mosaic on the wall, a voice emanating from the centre explaining the relic that greeted them.

"A human bestowed with the power of the gods, with the help of his nephew and his cunningness, Herakles defeated the mighty Hydra."

"A god amongst humans, Krishna used his powers to humble the mighty Kaliya."

"Any more questions? I would love to clear any doubts you may have on this rich, historic country of Greece. Additional information can be found on my podcast; if you want to check it out it's 'Alexandra's A-'

"Buy one *souvlaki* wrap, get another free!" A cry echoed from the distance.

The next few moments were a blur. Previously numb, sombre tourists were invigorated to the core, broken out of their stupor by the call for food - free food.

Who could blame them?

The horde moved in unison, making a beeline towards the voice, throwing dust in their wake.

When all had settled, all that remained was the dejected tour guide and Shiv.

He could finally take a good look at her. Golden hair tucked neatly behind a cap, a notebook and a booklet in hand, she looked around the same age as him. With a smart, green polo shirt and beige shorts, there was no mistaking her job.

Her piercing green eyes finally left the floor and met Shiv's, a grin tinged with sadness playing across her face.

"'Sup?"

The pair spent the next hour walking along the riverside, gradually opening up from their respective shells. Alexandra's boisterous laughs cut through the night's silence sporadically. Family, hobbies, pets, favourite artists - casual conversation was made as the sun ended its journey, sinking beneath the mountains. Finally, they sat on the bank, silence slowly creeping back in; the mood was suddenly sombre as wistful thinking entered the air.

"It really sucks, you know?"

Alexandra's pebble bounced once, twice, before sinking into the river, ripples swaying the weeds.

"Papu is sick, I can't pay bills, and I can't even keep a tour group together too," she whispered, close to tears.

"Hey hey now, keep that all aside. You'll get through it." Shiv had never been good at cheering others up, or talking for that matter, so he wrung his hands and waited for the worst.

"Yeah you're right, leave all that. So, what brings you to Athens?"

"I'm a first-year student at the National University of Athens here, and I honestly love this city. The history, the culture, all of it."

"Oh! So do I! I do the tour guide thing on the side because I love mythology and I need the extra money, you know?"

All of a sudden, the blanket of sadness had lifted. The two had found common ground.

"I've always been interested in mythology. The wisdom, the richness of the characters and the values they bring - I love the tales of old," Alexandra exclaimed, turning towards Shiv.

"Same here! My grandma used to quieten me down with tales from Indian folklore and of the gods - I would never get bored of them," Shiv eagerly responded.

"Those really were the times, not a worry in the world and your mind the playground for Herakles, Zeus - the whole lot," she sighed, sinking into the grass.

Moments passed in silence.

"I was listening to your explanation of the Hercules mosaic - you really know a lot," Shiv started.

"Hercules really was a character, right? The twelve labours - oh I've memorised them - none of them compare to him cleaning the stables of -"

"Augeas! I know right! Only labour which he used his brain and brawn, " she interjected, giving an apologetic grin.

"Damn, you really know your mythology huh," Shiv chuckled.

"Guess I do - a nerd to the core."

"No, no, I'm not complaining. I finally have someone to geek out with for mythology."

Alexandra tucked a curl behind her hair, grinning and staring at the water.

"So um, I was going to go to the temple of Herakles, Sunday 7AM, just to explore and, you know, enjoy the view. Wanna come?" Her eyes met his - 2 green wells.

"Yeah sure, I'll be there," Shiv said, a bit too quickly.

He had found someone like him, so why not make the most of it?

❧❧❧

"Up here!"

Shiv peered right into the morning sun, wincing in agony.

"Here, man," Alexandra giggled as she approached him, expertly navigating the rock strewn hillside.

"Making me wake up so early in the morning," grumbled Shiv, desperately rubbing his eyes to remove the dancing spots.

"Well, if you wanna enjoy the temple without wailing babies, this is the best time to do so," she said with a grin.

"This place is amazing. Where do we even start?"

It truly was. Undisturbed flora and the atmosphere of millenia-old relics gave a sense of unfettered calmness.

Located on the outskirts of the city, however, the temple hadn't aged well. All that remained on the hilltop were 3 crumbling columns, cracks racing across each side. Chunks of the temple littered the grassy floor, weeds fighting to survive in between cracks.

"Because of a lack of historical clues, no one knows the exact age of this temple. The only clue left behind was a small inscription - the only readable word saying "Herak", hence the name. Barely anyone comes here though - there's no point taking pictures with a couple of rocks," Alexandra informed Shiv, patiently waiting for him to catch up.

On the climb up to the columns, Alexandra slowly guided Shiv up the steep hillside, talking nonstop.

"Every now and then, I get this urge to find something, something others couldn't see, something about the secrets of this temple. There must be more to it," she said through short huffs - it was a difficult climb.

Shiv, out of breath and gasping desperately for more, could barely manage a nod. *This temple better be worth it*, he thought silently.

Reaching the top, the pair walked silently through the rubble, taking it all in, feeling the history at their feet. Thousands of years of festivals, gatherings, and just plain human life had seen this same view with prayers, wishes and desires of their own, now lost to the currents of time. All that remained of their presence was a broken shell of the temple's glory, now home to weeds and wildlife.

Shiv took a deep breath and let it out slowly. The view of Athens in the distance - a sprawling collection of dots - and the ancient, heavy atmosphere of history he was now part of: it was all beautiful.

Turning to her, Shiv had a wide smile on his face. "Thank you for bringing me here, I've never seen or felt anything like this before."

"My pleasure. It's nice to finally bring a friend along to appreciate these things."

They chatted for long: discussing college life, the best places to eat and the latest pop news. Between their conversation and strolling through the ruins, neither noticed the darkness creeping onto the sky.

As they walked together, approaching a column, Shiv tripped and was sent sprawling to the ground.

"Shit! You ok?" Alexandra rushed to his side, creases lining her forehead.

"Yea yea I'm fine; I should watch where I'm going," Shiv chuckled, rubbing his knee while gingerly poking at the blood blooming.

"Hey what's this?"

His fall had uncovered a small crevice, a peculiar-looking stone nestled deep within.

Delicately carved, a peacock's feather rested on the face of this smooth stone, sheltered from man and wind for a long time. Smaller than a palm of the hand, it lay there in a slumber.

"Gimme your hand, I'll try and take this stone out," said Shiv as curiosity got the better of him.

Holding her hand, Shiv reached into the hole, fingers clawing at empty space desperately.

At last, his fingers brushed the stone.

"Please don't go, my son. Only pain awaits you, just stay with me."

A grainy, black-and-white scene played out in front of Shiv's eyes; his whole world had transformed. It was as if he was stuck in a tape recording.

His own body was now pure mist, shifting in and out of form. On his left, he could see Alexandra, still holding his hand, eyes glued to a scene running unperturbed ahead. He tried touching the walls of the cavern they were in, to no avail - his hands just passed through. They were just spectators now - voiceless spirits.

A few feet up front were a young, tall man and a woman wrapped in shawls; the mother was desperately pleading with her son to heed her words. Rays of brilliance and light emanated from the man's chest - he was a figure of confidence. The mother, old age chipping away her face through wrinkles, was close to tears - her pleas were falling on deaf ears.

But it was the flickering that was interesting. Though the two remained the same, every few seconds their faces would distort and flicker between identities. The man had the same proud, confident expression, but flickered from a face with gold earrings and a moustache to a clean shaved face with flowing hair. The woman had the same pleading, maternal love written over her face, but flickered between a face with a *bindi* - a coloured dot on her forehead - and a nose ring, and a face with startling blue eyes.

The distortion in their forms - *were they holograms?*

"Ma, listen to me. I have never fallen in battle and I never shall. The gods above will watch over me and grant me victory. I have to go," the man stated, his figure flickering more by the second.

"*Karna*, I understand but I have a bad feeling about this. Please, just stay with your ma," the lady begged, her nose ring swayed as she shook her head.

The holograms were changing forms rapidly, the figures a blur. The hologram now resembled the man with the flowing hair.

"Do you forget? I am invulnerable. With this gift from the gods, nothing or no one can touch *Achilles*," the man proclaimed to the sky, his flowing hair riding the wind.

The man turned to Shiv, finally acknowledging his presence, and took a step towards him. Now he could see the full form of the hologram before him - one second he was Karna, the other second he was Achilles.

Gold armour encircled the figure in the hologram, fusing into his very body, light pouring relentlessly - as if the very sun powered it. He was ready for war, a bow, a quiver, and a sword completing the outfit. By now, both faces were a blur. Distorted yells of 'Achilles' and 'Karna' filled the air, rising in volume till it was too much.

Suddenly, the hologram's eyes went slack. The brilliance died, the yells were silenced, and his body crumpled to the ground. Waves of sorrow and anguish hit Shiv - his heartbeat doubled in tempo. The world started spinning, the cavern was crumbling; everything had become fast-paced. The lady ran to the motionless body, wailing, cursing the gods above, but to no avail.

The invulnerable demigod had fallen.

With a sharp intake of breath, Shiv sat up, panting in a frenzy.

He looked at his arms, his legs, the ruins around him, the wild weeds tickling his feet - he was back at the temple. The start contrast in colour, compared to the black-and-white world, hurt his eyes. He felt his body - it was normal again.

He began to calm down - began to process what had just happened.

Still holding his hand, Alexandra lay beside him, staring into the darkening sky with blank eyes, mouth agape.

"What just happened?"

"Hell if I know," Shiv whispered as he stood up. He started drifting aimlessly within the ruins, playing through what had just happened.

"Who is Karna?"

Shiv slowly came to a stop and smiled a sad smile.

"A demigod abandoned at birth by his mother, and raised as a lowly charioteer's son who found him by the river. A skilled warrior, unaware of his true lineage. From birth, his father, the sun god, had blessed him with impenetrable armour that would save him from any harm. But when a war came, he had to go, he had to go support his friends, no matter how evil they were. His mother pleaded with him not to go - though she knew it wasn't her son, she cared for him as one. During the war, he was tricked to take off his armour and eventually died alone. His birth mother only saw him, only felt his touch, at his funeral."

Crickets chirped at an incessant rhythm.

"So he's like Achilles then. A demigod, one of the most skilled warriors in their era, forced to head to war for their friends. Both were confident with their impenetrable skin. Both of their mothers pleaded for them not to go, fearing for their lives, but they believed nothing could bring them down. But down they both fell."

As Alexandra finished, Shiv sat down with her again, picking up the stone that had caused all this and turning it in his hands.

"It's beautiful, isn't it?"

The peacock feather had been chiselled with great detail. Otherwise, it was a normal piece of stone. What had happened when he had touched it? Why had they seen what they just saw?

"It was like a recording, wasn't it? Black and white and grainy. Oh and the scene, it was what we just said. A mother pleading with Karna or Achilles not to go to war. Did we just witness the legend?"

"The similarities between the two, it's just too much to brush aside. There must have been a reason we saw that."

"Who knew Indian and Greek mythology were so similar?"

Walking down the hill in confused silence, Shiv clutched at the stone, holding it to his chest as if his life depended on it.

Alexandra and he had experienced something outside of this world, outside of anything anyone had ever experienced. No one would even believe them, it was pointless to try. Only they could know about this.

The grainy recording, the man's proud expression, the light pouring from his body, the yells of their names - it kept playing through his head like a reel.

They were now in the realm of legends.

"And as you can see here, the force that the object applies..."

The professor's voice had reduced to a monotone, indistinguishable flow of words, sailing high above Shiv's ears. His mind was somewhere else, like it had been the past week, ever since that day at the Temple of Herakles. He couldn't get it out of his head no matter how hard he tried. It kept playing on a loop, the mother's wails pierced his dreams at night.

"Be prepared for tomorrow, I'll have a short quiz on..."

His grades on a steady descent, his room a mess, his friends maintaining their distance - he had to settle his mind before it consumed him. He needed to finish what was started.

"Oh and here of course, we have the..."

Alexandra trailed off, spewing whatever came to her mind, but deep down she knew it was all rambling. She had no idea what she was saying. Even her job had been affected by last Sunday.

That day had opened more questions than answers, and she found it hard not to think of Karna and Achilles and the mother and the yells and the -

Shit. Once she started thinking, it was a rabbit hole from there. The grainy, black and white world flashed in her eyes sporadically, making her wince to the confusion of her clients.

Several of them were frowning, as if they'd caught on. She really needed to get her act together.

Just then, her phone vibrated.

"8PM, Rizari Square" - a message from Shiv.

Guess I'll get it together tonight, she thought with a chuckle.

❧❧❧

"Sup?"

Alexandra smiled - déjà vu had just hit her.

With the same dishevelled hair and goofy grin, Shiv ambled towards her. But one thing was new. A line of forehead creases dotted his expression, making her want to squish them away.

"So..." he started, fidgeting with his hands as he spoke.

"What do we do now? Every day and night since then I've not been able to sleep in peace, study well or just focus on anything. We can't just ignore what we saw, there must be something for us to do. I can't rest till it's done."

"I mean, I've been thinking the same thing to be honest. Tour groups after tour groups I've just left confused and unhappy cause my minds just been elsewhere. Karna and Achilles - their names still ring in my head!" Alexandra plopped onto the grass, glaring at the soil.

"That whole flashback or recording or whatever - I think the main thing was the flickering forms. I mean it showed us how both Karna and Achilles were so similar right?"

"Yeah. I've never seen anything like it."

"But now we don't have any leads. We can't just search every shrine or temple in Greece can we."

Despair settled on their faces. The duo laid on the grass and mulled for what seemed like eternity.

"Are there any temples or shrines to Achilles nearby?" Shiv suddenly asked, sitting up straight, with palpable excitement.

"There's one on the outskirts, but no one really goes to-"

"Perfect! How about we go there tomorrow 7AM?" Shiv was almost bouncing from anticipation.

"Sure, but why?"

"If the flashback showed us Achilles, I'd say the most logical thing would be to visit his shrine and find another clue, correct?"

"Oh wow! Who knew you were so smart?" Alexandra chuckled.

Fixing a fake frown on his face, Shiv sulked as Alexandra laughed into the night.

❧❧❧

As they got closer, the nearby trickling of a stream could be heard. Hidden deep within vegetation and only accessible by a long hike, the shrine had few visitors. But the scenery made up for it.

Shrouded within tall trees lay the Shrine of Achilles, worn down throughout the centuries. It was a small shrine, a modest ode to one of the greatest heroes in Greek mythology.

The remnants of four central pillars and a courtyard were all that was there to be seen. The nearby stream and millenia of rain had eroded a lot of the statues and columns, resulting in indistinguishable heaps of carved stone. Green moss lay on every exposed rock, claiming the shrine as its own. Cracked stones littered the damp floor. The shrine hadn't aged well.

At first glance, nothing seemed out of the ordinary. But who knew what lay deep within the ruins.

Shiv and Alexandra spent the next two hours combing through the site, hoping to spot the all-too-familiar smooth stone. The dense canopy provided them some respite, but the sweltering heat made the stream more and more attractive by the second. No stone had been left unturned and no crack had been unexamined, but nothing had been found. Round and round they went, eyes darting for treasure. Mounting frustration was palpable in the air. *Was this a dead end?*

Out of breath and out of motivation, Shiv sat by the stream, feet dangling in the cool water. He peered up to the swaying branches and closed his eyes in defeat. Where had he gone wrong?

His swaying legs slowly caused a storm in the water, a brown murkiness spreading fast. Like the kid he was, a momentary smile played across his face as he continued to kick his legs with more gusto now. The whole river bed was being displaced, dirt being tossed into the current. Eventually, sadness creeped back in and he lay back on the grass. He peered at Alexandra, still scrutinising every nook and cranny, beads of sweat running down her red face. He had half the mind to tell her to stop, there wasn't any point.

The dust had settled down slowly. As Shiv sat back up and stared at his reflection in the still water, pondering, a glint caught his eye. Disturbed in his ruckus was a round, smooth stone, half buried. A carving was barely visible - a sun dawning, its rays wide and great. Karna's symbol.

"Alexandra!"

Woah.

The grainy black-and-white world; their bodies reduced to wisps of smoke. They were finally back.

But they were no longer in the previous flashback's setting. High on a bare mountain top, they could see a hellish world beneath. Rivers flowed in turbulent torrents, crashing into the jagged rocks strewn as far as the eye could see. Wails of agony ringed across the massive cavern, echoing from every corner. Shiv could just make out dark, hazy winged creatures soaring high, their cackles just reaching his ear and sending shivers down his spine.

Even though he was now just a mere spirit, he could feel the humidness, the infernal heat sucking out moisture, hopes, dreams and his desire to live.

"Kólasi." *Hell.* Shiv saw Alexandra shiver, despite the heat, out of the corner of his eye as she uttered those words.

The sole path they were on led to a round courtyard, centred around a throne. A throne encrusted with earth's most precious metals - and with skulls. A throne fit for the God of the Underworld.

With the only path being forward, Karna and Alexandra walked towards the throne, the air getting heavier by the second. At last they arrived, at a scene they would never forget for the rest of their lives.

"Here he is, my Lord."

In front of the throne lay a pale ghost, trembling incessantly. It resembled a king, a pot bellied man with a lopsided crown on his bald head. What was striking was the deep gash on his neck, a memento of his end on Earth. He was awaiting judgement.

Growling at the spirit was a massive hound - a hologram. Within that single form, it kept flickering between twin dogs, and a single massive three-headed dog. The hounds continued to drool and bare its canines at the ghost. Their long claws clacked against the floor at a steady rhythm as they paced in front of the throne. Click. Click. Click. Click. Click.

Surrounding the courtyard, hovering, were winged beings, guarding and watching the procession. Their forms flickered just like the hounds - holograms switching identities. One second they were men, dark skinned and fanged; with baleful eyes staring forward, a sword and a pair of wings, they exuded terror. The next second they were women, fair and fanged, with glittering eyes fixed ahead. A pair of wings, talons, and a leering expression didn't help Shiv's trembling body. He had to hold everything back to not run away. As they flickered between forms, their impatient growling and batting of wings never ceased. It was clear they were the guardians of this Hell. But what scared Shiv more was the fact that these monsters themselves, were mere servants of the hologram on the throne - the king of them all.

He was clearly the one in command. A seven foot man filled the seat, his pitch black complexion shifting and swirling like a never ending storm. Only a simple cloth over his lap covered his toned physique. The air seemed to distort around him as his appearance transformed ceaselessly.

Four arms protruded from his torso, and a garland ringed his neck. A mace and a sword in two, a noose and a staff in the other. His face was impassive, not betraying any emotion whatsoever. A sunken face with a mighty moustache. He commanded respect; the very air around him followed his bidding. "*Yama*," Shiv whispered.

The hologram shifted faces. Now on the throne laid a middle-aged man, adorned with a helmet and a toga. In one hand he sported a bident, in the other he petted his hound. A thick beard completed his impassive expression, blank yet focused. Inscrutable but all knowing. He commanded respect; the very air around him followed his bidding. "*Hades*," Alexandra whispered.

At last, the gods' eyes peered down at their feet, where the ghost cowered.

"You have lived your life, cut short by your own people. Your deeds have been read: stealing, abusing, tricking, using the people under you. Your vices outweigh your virtues." He declared, the hologram's form shifting at a rising speed.

"You have only given pain and suffering to your subjects," Hades said. His deep voice carried weight of its own, each word uttered booming into Shiv's very spirit. Realisation dawned in the spirit's eyes.

The holograms were changing forms rapidly, the figures a blur. The hologram now resembled the god with four arms.

"Now pain and suffering shall be given to you, morally deemed by your actions." Yama remained impassive as he uttered the ghost's fate.

The hologram shifted his gaze to his servants, who cackled in glee as they swooped down from the air and carried away the wailing spirit deep down into the depths of the Underworld. His cries faded into the distance and silence ruled the courtyard once again.

A sudden chill settled on the back of Shiv's spine.

The hounds' glaring eyes had now settled on him and Alexandra, drooling and snarling at the trespassers. They started to growl, deep from their throats - the growl got louder and louder until it was unbearable. The cavern started shaking, the mountain began to crumble, until their feet gave way. Falling, falling.

Falling.

With a sudden gasp, Shiv sat up, panting. He patted the ground and tugged at the grass to ease away the sense of plummeting. He looked around, frantically reassuring himself that he was back at the shrine. At last the fear began to subside, the knot in his stomach untying itself slowly. Alexandra had already recovered, lost in a state of pensiveness as she swayed her legs in the stream. Shiv picked himself up and approached her slowly, unsure of what to say.

"This one was really something else, wasn't it?" Alexandra said as she peered up at Shiv, her expression inscrutable.

"Terrifying wouldn't do it justice. Was that actually..."

"Hell. The Underworld. The Furies, Hades, Cerberus - the whole gang was there. We saw the judgement of a soul take place while the rivers beneath clashed against the hellish land below. There's no mistaking it. We just saw the Land of the Dead. Maybe my ...," she trailed off, hesitant to speak. *Her grandpa*, Shiv thought. Sick and dying, memories of her grandpa had started to fill Alexandra's head.

"Nevermind that. The flickering in each hologram was intense in this one, right?" She brushed it aside, desperate to change topics.

"Yeah. The *Furies* and the *Yamadutta's* were one - agents of Hades and agents of Yama I'm pretty sure. Winged, fanged, and followed the bidding of the God of the Underworld and Death. Even the dogs. Yama had twin dogs, I'm forgetting their names, and Hades had *Cerberus* - all merged into one hologram. Both guardians and beloved pets of the King himself." The chill he had felt back then was still a fresh, raw memory. He was grateful for the warmth of the sunlight here.

"Hades, or Yama, or whatever - you saw the way he judged the soul right? Both righteous and unbiased and impassive, sending ghosts wherever they rightly belong based on their past deeds. That messed up king went to the deepest depths of Hell, I'm sure."

"I mean yeah, but the similarities don't stop there. Both have jet black skin and are one of the oldest deities in their respective religions. Similar pets, similar servants, similar sense of justice. They really are alike," Shiv trailed off, lost in thought.

"But this flashback thing was something else. It felt too real. Nothing like the first one. And the things we're learning - they must be there for a reason right? All I'm seeing is how weirdly similar these figures from both mythologies or religions are."

"Right. But there must be more of this, there must be some end," Shiv got up with renewed energy, desperate to find it.

"Where's the nearest Hades temple?"

Alexandra stared at him like he'd lost his mind.

"The Greeks never built temples for Hades, idiot. A shrine to him, a Ploutonion, was often built near places with poisonous gases. There's one north of here, just 20 kilome-."

"What are we waiting for, let's go!" Shiv made his way down, tripping on every fallen branch in his radius.

Sighing, Alexandra followed him, grumbling.

"I better watch after him before he kills himself."

CHAPTER THREE

The End

"Welcome, to the Ploutonion of Eleusis," Alexandra presented in her best tour guide voice, squinting ahead. Shiv stood behind, marvelling the ancient history ahead of him.

"From the 6th century BC, this site has seen millennia of humans, priests, commonfolk, generals, soldiers - people of all walks of life - worship or respect this land. Now all that remained for archeologists to probe was rubble and stone."

"Nerd," Shiv whispered, to which he got a smack for.

Located in the Thracian plain, sparse shrubbery, rock and dirt on mountainsides summed up the view surrounding the Ploutonion.

Just to his left, Shiv could make out a large cave, sheltering the remains of a rectangular temple, remnants of the once impressive carved stone strewn around. Few walls and tiles had survived the test of time. A deep pit to the right was prominent and inescapable to the eye, rumoured to have held ritualistic activity in the past.

The once grand shrine to Hades and site for famous rituals had been reduced to a collection of indistinguishable, broken pillars, tiles and stone. *But this once revered, bustling shrine has the next key for their journey, I'm sure,* Shiv thought.

"Let's start searching, shall we?"

"There's nothing here."

Dust streaked across both of their faces, the sun beat upon them relentlessly, and mosquitos gnawed incessantly. The last 2 hours had been spent analysing every rock, every tile, every broken pillar - but no smooth stone was there.

"No stone anywhere. Would help if I knew the symbol we were looking for," Alexandra grumbled.

"The last one showed its something to do with the Indian counterpart of the previous flashback. So a symbol for Yama. Mace, buffalo, sword - all these can be a symbol for him. Even I'm lost," Shiv groaned.

Was this it? Two flashbacks and that's it? Was he meant to go back to college, never to find out the meaning of all this? He kicked at the ground. This wasn't like him, but he was so, so close that he let his emotions run rampant.

He got up and walked along the caves, pacing back and forth to vent it all out. His hands ran alongside the walls, bouncing on every uneven part. He wasn't getting anywhere.

Suddenly, he stopped

"What happened?"

Retracing his steps, he let his hand rest on what he had just felt. It had felt weird, something different from the rest of the carvings. A deeply chiselled vertical line, connected to a circle.

At first, he was lost. *Was he overthinking it?*

A noose.

Shiv slapped his head and beckoned Alexandra over with all the energy he could muster.

"I present to you, the noose!" Shiv exclaimed with a wide grin.

"Huh. Have you finally lost your mind?"

"No *pa*, the noose is another one of Yama's symbols. They say it always follows anyone and takes your soul when it's time. We saw it in his hand in the flashback, remember!?"

"Damn, that's deep. But it's not a smooth pebble this time..."

"I don't know why, but this is our best bet."

"And if you're touching it, why's nothing happening?"

"Oh that. We have to hold hands when we touch it, remember?"

Shiv had no clue why, but at this point he wasn't complaining.

Alexandra rolled her eyes in mock disgust as Shiv's fingers brushed against the carving.

Thunder greeted them back into the black and white world.

Shiv and Alexandra were hovering mid air this time, their wispy form fighting to stay afloat in the strong wind. It was dark, nothing could be made out. Yet.

A boom echoed beneath.

Arcs of lightning started dancing across the sky, casting an eerie glow on the scene playing beneath them. Now Shiv could see them. And he would continue seeing them every sleepless night.

A battle ensued below. No ordinary battle, however. A battle between two. Their blows shook the earth, their yells reverberated incessantly, and their forms nothing like a mortal's.

On Shiv's left, lay a monster. A monster whose head seemed to brushed the stars and whose width seemed to span an ocean. Brief flashes of lightning could only reveal so much of him, painting his scaly skin in a pale white glow. The flickering of his forms, masked by the darkness, chilled Shiv to the very core. Though he knew he was safe, that he was a mere spirit in this world, fear plagued his mind as every fibre of his body yelled at him to run.

The monster was humanoid from the waste up - as human as it could be. Long flowing hair, a ragged beard and fangs, the size of mountains, made up his face, contorted with rage. His eyes - Shiv couldn't look at them for too long. The pupils were pitch black, devoid of emotions or humanity. His torso, massive and scaled, shadowed the land beneath. He was already the stuff of nightmares. But below his waist, his body morphed into snake coils, writhing and destroying acres in its wake. Wings. A pair of pitch black wings, beating and creating storms, camouflaged into the night. Fire darted from his eyes as he bared his fangs and roared.

Typhon. The Greek father of all monsters.

All of a sudden, darkness ruled again as the lightning dimmed. The monster faded in the darkness.

Boom. A clap of thunder signalled the hologram switching forms.

The wings had disappeared, and a massive crown rested on the monster's head. But the rest was the same. He bared his chest to the heavens and roared.

Vritra. The Indian serpent of Chaos.

Both were personifications of drought and chaos, monsters who terrorised the gods. And the only one who managed to subdue them was the god, and his 2 faces, who was fighting them now.

He was tiny in comparison to his foe. But he had already managed to do some damage - smoking craters could be seen on the monster. The god was his own source of light, electricity crackling and bouncing off his skin. With every flick of his hand, lightning arced from the sky and blasted the monster, drawing out yells of agony. A rod, shaped like a thunderbolt, was held steadfast, humming and slowly increasing its vibration. The final attack was about to come.

He resembled a man in his 60s, a flowing white beard and moustache riding the wind. His chiselled body clung tightly to his white toga. But his holographic form was flickering rapidly like the others - two men merging into one.

He shifted into a younger man, muscular and encased in golden armour. A gold crown accompanied his clean shaved face, fixed in an expression of determination. A bright red mark adorned his forehead. It was time to finish the monster off.

As Shiv squinted, agape, the god slowly rose in the air, the flickering unbearable to watch now. The metal thunderbolt was hoisted in his arms, humming at a deafening level now. Electricity danced and lightning rumbled over the bolt - his final and most powerful weapon.

A brief expression of unease clouded the monster's face, but it passed by quickly. With all of its gargantuan might, it lunged. Wind and land rose with it, looming over the seemingly small god.

The heavens held their breath.

With a roar, the god flung the master bolt. Arcing through the air, collecting charge as it flew through, it hit the monster in its chest. The rod exited through the other side, leaving a sizzling crater through its heart. The embers in its eyes died down as the monster came crashing, sending shockwaves for miles.

A sudden quiet descended upon the decimated valley, and sunlight filtered back in. The hologram summoned his bolt back, and sat. Now Shiv and Alexandra could see the cuts racing across his body, deep. He was lost in thought as his face flickered between each god.

With a sigh, he snapped his fingers.

What the. It still isn't over?

The scene had changed. But they weren't back in the real world. The same old grainy black-and-white images played out in front of them.

This is new.

Shiv and Alexandra now stood in a throne room. 12 ivory white columns bordered the room and the sky was the ceiling. Lit braziers were the only furniture present. There was nothing but empty air on the sides. The throne room was in the sky, nestled in clouds. *Was this...*

The hologram of the 2 gods had appeared now, sitting comfortably in the central throne. The biggest throne of them all. Fit for the king of them all.

To his right lay a cup, and as he chugged from it, his cuts seem to close and heal. *Nectar?* Shiv had growing suspicion on who the man was, and it wasn't helping settle his mind.

The crown, the central throne, the lightning. He was the king. The king of the gods.

Zeus.

Indra.

The flickering had lulled, but the forms still shifted between the 2 faces. The man yawned up at the sky, and as his eyes came down, they settled on Shiv and Alexandra.

"My, my, my. What do we have here?"

9 798888 331644